What's that weed?

by Russ Hudson

illustrated by Avijit Bhowmick

For Stella. For everyone.

"What's that weed?"
asked Emmy Lynn Watson, all dressed in tweed,
as she pointed to strange flower buds
that were bursting with seeds.

"That's not a weed, it's called marijuana,"
replied Stella Davina, daughter of the farmer.
"We plant it each year — it grows on our farm,
everyone loves it; especially my mom."

"But what does it do — is it food that you eat?"
asked Emmy Lynn Watson, the new kid on the street.
She looked to her friend Stella, her neighbor on Dunn Road,
then brushed off a bug from her tweed-colored clothes.

"Yes, you can it eat, of course; that's for sure!
You can eat it, and drink it, and smoke it, and more!"

Stella stopped then, just long enough,
to grab some seeds from the tops of the buds.
Then into her mouth, she popped them by ones
and twos, and threes; then she started to run.

"C'mon Emmy," Stella said with a grin,
"I'll show you all the things we use marijuana in."

Just across the yard was a fence with a gate
Where a half-dozen chickens pecked, pooped, and played
And there on a post hung a bag full of seeds
Where Stella reached in and said, “Hey Emmy, take these!”

Then Emmy in tweed helped give the chickens their feed
While Stella explained, "But these aren't just any old seeds!
These are the seeds that come from marijuana;
It's a super food, that's for sure, as healthy as water!"

Then into the house the girls raced as they laughed,
stopping when they came upon Stella's dad.
In a big wooden chair, with a book where he sat,
a strange apparatus perched in his lap.

“Hello, girls,” he said with a smile,
“I’m taking a break to read for a while.”
And then with a flash and flick of his wrist,
he brought forth a lighter, and a glass pipe to his lips.

“That’s called a bong,” said Stella, to Emmy in tweed,
“some people use one if they like smoking weed.”

"My dad likes beer, is it sort of like that?"
asked Emmy Lynn Watson, in a tweed-patterned hat.

“It sure is,” said Stella, who then hugged her dad, “people use all different things to relax.”

**Leaving the father with his book and his weed,
the girls went to the kitchen; it was almost time to eat.
There on the table, on plates colored white,
were jagged-leaf salads, and forks, spoons, and knives.**

**"Those salads look weird —
are they leaves from your weeds?"
Emmy crossed her arms in their tweed-colored sleeves.**

"Well, they're not really weeds, if they're good enough to eat.
Cannabis leaves give us the greens that we need!"

Then as if to prove her claim right away, Stella snuck two big weed leaves from the white-colored plates.

One leaf for Stella and one for Emmy Lynn, then off the girls went with green-tinted grins.

They left the warm kitchen with its table and chairs,
Swallowing weed bits as they hiked up the stairs.
Down the hall to see Stella's sister June,
They knocked on the door to the older girl's room.

“Hello sister, can Emmy and I come in?”
And soon enough, June beckoned from within.
“Sorry to bug you, we’ll be fast, you’ll see;
I just want to show Emmy the honey you need.”

Stella's sister June took a jar from her desk,
then held it to the light to show inside the glass.
"This is weed honey, it keeps me seizure-free;
I use it to treat my epilepsy."

"Wow!" said Emmy, her eyes growing large,
"This is made from those plants on your farm?"
"Yup; it's called cannahoney, and we make it right here
It keeps me out of the hospital, year after year."

Back down the hall to where her brother played guitar
In a cozy apartment above the garage for their cars
There they all sat, where brother Fred brought them drinks
He took out a dropper and against his glass it clinked.

"What's that?" said Emmy, her brow slightly raised
"Oh!" said Fred, "this treats anxiety from my military days
It's called cannabis tincture, and it helps my PTSD
it aids me in dealing with the bad things that I've seen."

**Amazed and intrigued, and all dressed in tweed,
Emmy Lynn Watson was learning a lot about weed.
As they went downstairs to the call of Stella's momma,
Emmy asked Stella "Why do you call it marijuana?"**

**Stella skipped happily and gave a small shrug;
"My mom calls it 'pot,' but my brother calls it 'nugs.'
My dad calls it weed, but he always tells me this:
The correct term is called 'cannabis.'"**

Into the kitchen the two girls did saunter,
Where momma pressed seeds on the butcher-block counter.
"Are those cannabis seeds?" Emmy asked with a lisp
Momma just laughed and smiled a 'yes.'

"We press our own seeds, and I don't mind the toil;
it's so much better than vegetable oil!"
Momma pressed the handle and the gold oil poured out,
Though there was one thing that Emmy could not figure out.

“But can’t you just buy it in any old store?”
Emmy, in tweed, politely implored.
“Not just yet,” momma said, “but one day real soon.
Now you girls wash up, and head to the dining room.”

They sat at the table as one family;
The parents, the kids, and Emmy in tweed.
And as she looked at each one in turn,
Emmy was surprised at all that she learned.

From eating to relaxing, oils and seeds,
To the life-saving treatment of epilepsy.
But there was still one question that Emmy didn't get,
So she asked her new friends just what it all meant;

"If cannabis is so great, and useful indeed,
Then why would anyone call it a weed?"

Pass
it
on
The End

About the Author

Russ Hudson is an international cannabis consultant and author. The main character in What's That Weed, Stella, is the author's daughter, and the events in the book are based loosely around life on the Hudson family's off-grid farm in Liberty, Maine, USA.

Mr. Hudson's recent autobiography, "Weed Deeds: From Seed to Sage," was published in June 2017, and is available on CreateSpace, Amazon, and Kindle. Hudson is also the founder and editor of www.MarijuanaGames.org, and www.CannaBizConsultant.com. To learn more about Russ, you can connect with him on Facebook or LinkedIn:

https://www.facebook.com/RussellJHudson
https://www.linkedin.com/in/russhudson/

COMING SOON FROM RUSS HUDSON!

Why Oh Why Do People Get High?

Join Stella and Emmy as they go on another fun-filled journey of alternative discovery, this time learning about the many different ways that normal people "get high," and why they do it.

LOOK FOR IT SOON!

CPSIA information can be obtained
at www.ICGtesting.com
Printed in the USA
LVHW07n2334230318
571034LV00012B/42/P

* 9 7 8 0 6 9 2 9 6 3 8 5 2 *